'*Major and Mynah* is a marvellous mystery with friendship, warmth, resilience and just a smidge of magic.'

Mo O'Hara

'A book to cheer, entertain and enable children, with or without hearing aids, everywhere!'

E.M. Watson, reviewer

'Karen Owen is a skilled storyteller!'

Sarah Todd Taylor

'*Major and Mynah* is engaging and fun, with beautiful and positive disability representation and a very sweet young heroine.'

Liam James, bookwormhole.co.uk

'Loved this fast-paced story about best mates, spies and a crime-fighting mynah bird!'

Cathy Cassidy

MAJOR and MYNAH

Karen Owen

Illustrated by Louise Forshaw

To, Lawrence,

Welcome to S.P.U.D!

Firefly

Karen Owen

First published in 2022
by Firefly Press
25 Gabalfa Road, Llandaff North, Cardiff, CF14 2JJ
www.fireflypress.co.uk

A CIP catalogue record of this book is
available from the British Library.

1 3 5 7 9 8 6 4 2

Print ISBN 9781913102746
ebook ISBN 9781913102753

This book has been published with the support
of the Books Council of Wales.

Typeset and design by Becka Moor

Printed and bound by CPI Group (UK) Ltd, Croydon,
CR0 4YY

To 'Polly' Sue, my childhood BFF

-KO

For anyone who has ever felt different

-LF

Super Perceptive Undercover Detectives
Agent Files

Name: Callie Major

Age: 9 ¾

Code name: CM1

Detective skills: Spying

Keeping secrets

Remembering names and interesting facts

Talents: Riding a bike

Super sprinting

Removing huge hairy spiders from the bath

Super Perceptive Undercover Detectives
Agent Files

Name: Grace Ambrose

Age: 9 years, 11 months, 2 days, 3.5
                      hours (at the time of writing)

Code name: GA1

Detective skills: Code breaking

                       Map drawing

                       Calculating numbers

Talents: Basketball

                      Bike riding

                      Reaching chocolate hidden on
                      the top shelf

The Mystery Begins

It all started with the mystery of two missing things.

The first thing to vanish was a silver mountain bike belonging to our neighbour, Mrs Moore.

'I only left it on the driveway for a minute or two,' she yelled over the garden fence. 'When I went back out it'd gone. Stolen!'

Mum shook her head in sympathy and promised we would keep our eyes peeled.

How do you peel eyes?

Then Mum discovered Luke's swimming trunks had disappeared from our washing line!

'I hope this isn't one of your jokes, Callie,' she said, frowning at me.

Maybe she was remembering the time I hid Luke's school tie in the freezer because he scoffed all the chocolate ice cream. But it wasn't me who took his trunks, and I think Dad was way too busy sawing wood in his workshop to have had time to play a joke.

'Maybe it was a werewolf? Or a ghost?' I suggested.

Mum rolled her eyes at me.

'Or they flew off?'

'There's no wind!' said Mum.

Which was true. I was eating breakfast in the garden because it was so hot.

Mum huffed and puffed and said everyone was going to be late unless she found them IMMEDIATELY. Luke burst into tears because he's five and that's what he does when things go wrong. Also, he was desperate to go on his swimming playdate with Kieran.

Straightaway I knew this would be an interesting case for SPUD to solve. SPUD is made up of me and Grace (my BFF) and it stands for Super Perceptive Undercover Detectives. We chose 'perceptive' because it's one of our teacher's favourite words. Mrs Manning says it describes someone who is good at seeing things. Detectives have to be very clever at spotting things other people don't see.

The SPUD crew already had a meeting planned for later today. We're inventing a code using our torches so we can communicate from our bedroom windows. We need a code because we're not allowed to use our mobile phones at home. They're only for EXTREME EMERGENCIES, to keep us safe and for if we get lost (which would be difficult in our village because it's so small and we know all the roads off by heart).

My belly moaned and I felt a teeny bit sick as I looked at my cereal. I knew why. Before I could meet Grace, Mum and I had to drop off Luke and then go to the hospital.

To collect the ear things.

I really, really didn't want to.

I'd taken so long to eat my cereal it'd gone soggy. As I spooned it out of the milk, a bird swooped down and landed on the table next to me. I jumped up in fright because it wasn't the sort of thing you expected to happen when you were eating your Rice Krispies. The bird was bigger than a robin but smaller than a crow, and it was black with yellow stripes on its head. It looked straight at me and chirped! How cute was that?

'Hello.' I felt a bit silly because I was talking to a wild bird that had no idea what I was saying. The bird was straggly and looked like it hadn't eaten for ages. It stared at me with brown watery eyes, then stared at my bowl, and stared back at me again.

Chirp!

I pushed my bowl of soggy cereal towards it. 'Have some breakfast.'

Chirp! Chirp! Chirp!

The bird jumped on to the edge of my bowl and dipped its orange beak into it. It slurped the milk and gobbled up the Rice Krispies.

Chirp! Chirp! Chirp!

It was so excited it hopped onto the rim of the bowl but then it slipped and fell in. Milk splashed all over the table as the bird flapped wildly. At first I laughed because it looked so funny but then I realised it was scared so I fished it out. It shook itself and its feathers stuck out like a spooked cat's fur.

'You're safe now,' I said.

Chirp!

The bird pushed its head into my hand and let me stroke it. I'd never done that before! Its head was soft and warm.

Luke whooshed into the garden pretending to be a space rocket. He was wearing his gruesome green *I'm An*

Alien! pants. The bird took one look and flew away.

'You scared the bird!' I snapped, but Luke ignored me.

'I'm going to wear my alien pants for swimming!' he announced to the whole world.

Then Mum shouted it was TIME TO GO, and my belly went into mad washing-machine tumbling all over again.

Spiders and Slugs

Mum and I sat in the hot waiting room. On the wall were loads of posters about hospital services and community support groups. I slouched on a chair with sponge sticking out from a split where so many people's bottoms had squashed it. I pointed at the sign on the wall:

Welcome to the ENT Department

'Enormous Naughty Tarantulas Department,' I said.

Mum rolled her eyes. Of course, I knew it really stood for Ear, Nose and Throat. I'd been here before to do a hearing test and it was a DISASTER. I had to sit in a metal box with mega-thick walls and wear huge headphones over my ears. Every time there was a beeping sound I pressed a button. Then they repeated the test but they played loads of whooshing sounds at the same time. The sounds were called white noise. I don't know why they're called white instead of yellow or purple. You try hearing tiny beeps when it sounds like a helicopter is taking off next to you.

Anyway, the doctor said my hearing wasn't good enough and that I needed hearing aids. I think I hear nearly everything but sometimes sounds get muddled up. It's worse if people mumble, which they do a lot. So I just guess. If there are loads of different noises then I can only hear the loudest one and the rest become a messy blur.

So, today we had to collect the hearing aids. I really didn't want them because I think they look ugly and I just know people will make fun of me. And by 'people', I mean certain people at school.

'Did you hear what I just said?' asked Mum.

'Err...'

'I said this is very exciting because you'll be able to hear. We won't have to keep repeating ourselves or have another saucepan incident,' said Mum.

I sighed. They haven't let me forget the time Dad stood at the bottom of the stairs and banged a saucepan with a wooden spoon because he was fed up with me not hearing him call that tea was ready.

Mum was talking about Mrs Moore's stolen bike and the mystery of Luke's missing trunks again. Of course, SPUD is top secret so I couldn't tell Mum that Grace and I were going to examine the scene for clues and speak to witnesses.

'Mrs Moore should have locked her bike so the thief couldn't steal it,' said Mum. 'You must remember to lock yours. I know it's boring but it's very important.'

'Yes, Mum, I know.'

I was more interested in thinking about the tame bird from breakfast. Maybe it was somebody's pet and had escaped through an open window while they weren't looking?

I wish I had a pet, one I could keep at home. I've got a donkey called Clarice, but I never get to see her because she lives a long way away in a rescue sanctuary. I used my Christmas money to sponsor her and I get sent photos and updates. I feed Harold – Mr and Mrs Moore's cat – when they go on holiday, too.

Mostly, I'd like a Chilean Rose tarantula. It's got a fiery-red back, hairy legs, eight eyes and two fangs. It's so beautiful. When I grow up I want to be a spider-ologist. If I had a pet spider then I'd be able to study it, but Mum and Dad have said

NO PETS ALLOWED!

This is because Mum is allergic to cats…

Dad said he hasn't got time to walk a dog…

There's no space for a fish tank…

And DEFINITELY NO SPIDERS!

…I wonder how they'd feel about a bird?

A smiley doctor came into the waiting room and called my name. My tummy tumbled madly again. If I was a giant house spider then I could have been out of there before anyone blinked. They can run up to half a metre PER SECOND. But I'm not a giant house spider, so I followed the smiley doctor.

Her office was very quiet. I sat down by her desk, which had a computer and lots of wires and medical-looking things that made my tummy whirl again.

'I'm very passionate about ears,' she said excitedly.

Or she might have said she was very passionate about chairs. I wasn't entirely sure because at that exact moment she put the new hearing aids in my ears!

Then she switched them on. Everything was SO loud. And squeaky. And…

'ARGHHH! Wasp!' I jumped out of my seat and flapped wildly.

The doctor ducked out of my way. 'It's not a wasp! It's the air-conditioning unit you can hear.'

Well, it sounded like a wasp to me.

Computers whirred.

Bracelets jangled.

Chairs squeaked.

'It'll take a little while, but you'll soon get used to the noise,' said the doctor. She showed me how to switch them on and use the different settings.

But the noise was even worse when we went outside to the car park.

Cars **REVVED**.

Brakes **SQUEALED**.

Horns **BEEPED**.

By the time we got home, I had the worst headache ever. It felt like a tyrannosaurus rex was breakdancing inside my head.

I hate the hearing aids. From now on I'm going to call them THE SLUGS because it feels like slugs have crawled into my ears and got stuck. I don't care what the doctor said about getting used to them. I'm never ever wearing them again!

A Close Call

Grace came round on her bike as soon as I got home from hospital. She chained it to the drainpipe even though her bike was in our back garden because crime prevention is very important. Mum gave us raspberries and ice cream and we went up to my bedroom.

Grace and I have been best friends since we played with the cookery set together at nursery – and now we're nearly ten! Grace is amazing with numbers and inventing codes, so she is the best person to sit next to in numeracy. Also, she's really kind because she knows how much I want a pet, so she lets me hold Fred (her white rabbit) and help to clean his hutch.

I pulled my box of secret things from its hiding place under my bed and unlocked it. Inside was our SPUD logbook.

'Ready to investigate our next case?' I asked.

But Grace wanted to see the Slugs first, so I took them out of their box and showed her.

'I think they look cool. They'll be great when you're being a spy!' Grace grinned.

I put the Slugs in so I could do a secret spy impression. Straight away, everything was so much louder. I heard Grace chewing raspberries and the laptop whirring and…

'BOO!'

'Boo what?' I asked Grace.

She looked at me like I was mad.

'You said "boo!"'

Grace laughed. 'No, I didn't!'

AARGGGHHHHHH!!! So now I was hearing imaginary sounds, too.

I took the Slugs out. I'd had enough of them for one day.

Grace gasped and pointed at the windowsill. My windows were wide open because of the heatwave, and the friendly bird from this morning was poking its head in. In the sunlight, its plumage shimmered green like jade.

'Hello again,' I said.

And the bird hopped inside!

Chirp!

Then it flew over to my desk where I'd left my raspberries and ice cream, which was starting to melt.

Chirp!

'You're hungry again?' I laughed.

Chirp! Chirp! Chirp!

Grace was confused so I told her about the soggy cereal and how the bird had slurped it all up. I held out my last raspberry and the bird jumped on to my hand. It nibbled and pecked until there was squashed raspberry everywhere.

'It's so cute,' said Grace.

'Mum will go mad if she sees it in here. You know how she feels about pets,' I said.

We didn't even know what type of bird it was, so we looked on the laptop to find out. After studying lots of pictures, we discovered it was a breed called a mynah.

TOP FIVE THINGS ABOUT
MYNAH BIRDS

1. They are <u>brilliant</u> at mimicking sounds
2. They can laugh and whistle
3. They are noisy and friendly but can be aggressive if they feel threatened
4. They love eating fruit, seeds, worms and insects (especially grasshoppers and blackcurrants)
5. They hate being in direct sunlight because their skin is so sensitive

Knock knock.

'It's me,' Mum announced, knocking on my door and coming in AT THE SAME TIME. What's the point of knocking if she doesn't wait for me to say come in?

Quick as a flash I scooped the mynah bird up in my hands and held it behind my back. Its beak nipped at my finger which tickled and I had to try really hard not to laugh.

'I've brought you some orange squash,' said Mum.

'Thank you,' Grace and I said at the same time.

Mum looked at us suspiciously. 'What are you doing?'

'I was showing Grace the Slugs,' I said, which was technically true.

Mum frowned. 'Your curtain is caught on the open window. It's going to tear.'

'I'll sort it,' I promised.

But I couldn't do it straight away for OBVIOUS REASONS … and Mum was on a mission to rescue the curtain.

Ring ring!

I gulped as I felt the bird's body vibrate while it mimicked a ringtone.

Mum looked surprised. 'Is that the phone?'

'Sounds like it,' I said. Which it sort of did, from really far away.

Ring ring!

'It is the phone!' Mum rushed out to answer it.

As soon as Mum left the room, Grace let go of the huge breath she had been holding. 'That was close!'

'Too close!' I brought the bird out from behind me.

Ring ring! Ring ring!

Ding - dong! Ding - dong!

SPUD CASE FILE: Missing Thing #1

Crime: Theft of Mrs Moore's mountain bike.

Location: Driveway of 22 Merton Way.

Description: Silver frame with a black seat. Adult's bike. Nearly new.

Action: Examination of scene for clues. Spoke to witnesses. No footprints or unusual sightings.

Suspects: Swimming trunk thief?

SPUD CASE FILE: Missing Thing #2

Crime: Theft of Luke's swimming trunks.

Location: Washing line in back garden at 20 Merton Way.

Description: Red with a blue stripe.

Action: Examination of scene for clues. Spoke to witnesses. No footprints or unusual sightings.

Suspects: ~~Werewolf.~~ ~~Ghost.~~ ~~Wind.~~ Mountain bike thief. Luke?

4

Too Much NOISE

The next day there was a new missing-thing mystery. This time it was at our school.

I didn't want to go to school at first because I'd had a huge row with Mum and Dad about the Slugs.

'I'm not wearing them,' I announced.

'You've got to,' said Dad. 'Otherwise you won't hear and then you won't learn.'

Grace and I always walk to school with our mums and Luke. They let us walk together a little bit in front of them which is great because it

means we can have private conversations without them hearing. We walked down Merton Way and along the road leading to our school.

'I can't believe how noisy it is today!' I told Grace.

Mr Carter's dog barked as loud as a lion.

A letterbox snapped shut like the jaws of a crocodile.

A lorry growled like a hungry dragon.

Then a police car whizzed past with its sirens and blue flashing lights and stopped right outside our school!

'Look!' I said to Grace. 'There's a huge hole in the fence around the school field.'

We rushed to the scene to investigate.

'What's happened?' I asked a police officer standing by the fence.

'A thief has stolen your school mower,' she said.

The lawnmower was like a mini tractor and the caretaker rode it around our large playing field to cut the grass.

'That mower is huge, so the thief needed to make a huge hole,' I said to Grace, who was busy taking notes. 'I wonder if it's the same thief who stole the bike and the swimming trunks?'

'We need a meeting of the SPUD after school,' Grace decided.

Which was all VERY EXCITING.

It was nearly time for school to start so the playground was really busy.

Jack and Finn's football thumped like a stomping giant.

Tamsin laughed like a squealing whistle.

Then the bell rang loudly and made me jump. It was time to line up with our class. We stood in front of Tamsin and Amber. Tamsin poked me in my back.

'What have you got stuck in your ears?' she said.

I covered my ears with my hands so she couldn't see the Slugs.

SQUEAK!

The high-pitched noise hurt my ears. Then I remembered the doctor had said that would happen if the microphones on the Slugs were covered up.

'You sound like an alien!' Tamsin did

a rubbish impression and loads of my class laughed.

I turned my back on her. Grace squeezed my hand.

'I wish my hair was longer,' I whispered to her. I'd spent ages in front of the mirror last night, trying to tug my hair over my ears. Then I'd looked up how long it takes for hair to grow. It grows an average of 1.25cm a month which is a TINY amount. That means it'll take until Christmas for my hair to cover up my ears and that's far too long to wait. I could wear a wig but the only one I've got is a clown's wig.

'You need to become famous. Then all your fans will copy you and get fake Slugs and they'll be cool,' said Grace.

Later, we were in the classroom reading nonsense poems on the whiteboard when there was a burning smell. A sign appeared:

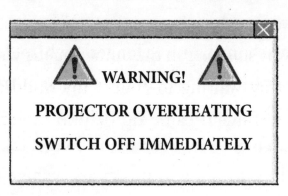

⚠ **WARNING!** ⚠

PROJECTOR OVERHEATING

SWITCH OFF IMMEDIATELY

Which was exactly what Mrs Manning was doing when…

BANG!

I jumped up off my chair so high it was probably a new world record. It turned out that the bulb in the projector had blown but because of the Slugs it sounded like a firework. I yanked them out but the whole class had seen and was staring at me.

The noise was even worse in the dinner hall because everyone was using what Mrs Manning calls their OUTDOOR voices, even though we were INDOORS.

I was standing in the dinner queue with my tray waiting to collect my pudding when Tamsin came up behind me and yelled ROAR right in my ear.

I jerked the tray and knocked over my cup of water. My lunch was ruined and there was gravy all over my dress. Tamsin and her friends laughed like it was the funniest thing ever. I shouted and she shouted back, and it ended with the dinner ladies marching both of us to Mrs Manning.

'It was a joke,' said Tamsin.

'It was a mean thing to do,' said Mrs Manning.

Tamsin claimed she was sorry but I saw her crossing her fingers behind her back so I knew she didn't really mean it. Then Mrs Manning sent her out to play which wasn't fair at all.

But really the Slugs were to blame because none of it would have happened without them. I yanked the Slugs out and threw them across the classroom. They hit the wall and fell behind the bookcase.

Mrs Manning didn't tell me off or huff and puff or anything like that. Instead, she pulled out the bookcase so she could reach behind it. Out came three zillion years of dust, a pencil sharpener, two felt-tip pens without their lids, a crumpled book, a dried-up apple core, and the Slugs.

'I wondered where that book had got to,' she said.

She brushed the dust off it and smiled at me. 'My dad's got hearing aids and it took him ages to get used to them. He said they gave him a headache for a while because everything was so much louder.'

'My head really hurts,' I admitted.

We talked for a little while and she finally agreed that I could take the Slugs out for the rest of the afternoon.

It was Dad's turn to collect me and Luke from school because Mum was at work, driving a coach somewhere. Mrs Manning told him what had happened. Afterwards, Dad overheard her talking to Tamsin's mum. He told me she'd said that Tamsin had been very unkind and she needed to think about her choices. That made me feel a bit better.

But I still HATE the Slugs.

SPUD CASE FILE: Missing Thing #3

Crime: Theft of school's tractor mower.

Location: Equipment shed at our school.

Description: Red with chunky black wheels and a black plastic seat and a steering wheel.

Action: Examination of scene for clues. Police said bolt cutters used to break fence. Spoke to witnesses. Mr Bryant (who lives opposite school) said he heard a strange noise in the night but thought it was foxes.

Suspects: None.

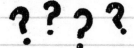

Gran's Birthday Card

We got home from school and then Dad remembered he'd forgotten to take me and Luke to the shop to buy a box of chocolates for Gran's birthday.

'I can go on my bike to the shop,' I offered. 'It's not very far and I'll be really careful.'

'So long as you wear your hearing aids so you can hear the traffic properly,' he said. 'Oh, and keep your mobile phone on and remember to lock your bike on the railings.'

I love riding my bike. Best of all is pedalling really hard and then going downhill because I feel like I'm flying. It only takes five minutes to cycle to the shops at the Market Square, and that's if you're going quite slowly. There's a Co-op shop, the chippie (where we buy fish and chips on special occasions like Mum and Dad being too tired to cook), the library, and a pharmacy.

I found Gran's favourite chocolates and bought the biggest box that I could afford with the money Dad gave me because she always shares them. Then I cycled back home again.

Dad looked puzzled. 'Where's the card?'

'What card?

'Gran's card. For her birthday,' he said.

'You didn't tell me to get a card. You said chocolates.' I know grown-ups get forgetful when they're older but, honestly, Dad is thirty-eight, not a hundred!

'I did! Clearly you didn't hear,' said Dad. Oops. I grabbed a pen and wrote

HAPPY BIRTHDAY GRAN

on the box of chocolates. Luke giggled but Dad didn't see the funny side of it. I offered to go back to the shop but Dad said I'd have to make a card, which was going to take ages. That annoyed me so I stomped down to the den which Grace and I had built behind Dad's workshop. We used an old tent with planks of wood to prop it up and it's my favourite place because lots of spiders have spun their webs there.

Ring ring!

It was the mynah bird, pretending to be a telephone again! Before I had a chance to say 'hello', a spider crawled out of a gap in the wood. It had a beautiful leaf-shaped pattern on its fat body which meant it was a type of orb spider. Suddenly the bird darted at it!

'No!' I grabbed an empty plant pot and covered the spider.

'Oi, that's my lunch!' said the bird.

'Not anymore!'

'But I'm hungry!' the bird moaned.

I stared at the bird.

The bird stared at me.

What…?

'You can talk!' I said.

'And you can hear me!' the bird replied.

This was SERIOUSLY WEIRD.

6

A Bird Called Bo

For the first time in my life, I was speechless. Mum and Dad would've said this was unbelievable because apparently I never stop talking.

'You're listening to me at last!' said the bird. 'I've been talking to you for ages.'

OK. I was tired and upset because of the drama with the Slugs.

Or my brain had been fried by the projector bulb explosion.

Or I was imagining things.

It had to be one of those because it's impossible for wild birds to talk. They're BIRDS!

The mynah ruffled its feathers and settled down on top of the plant pot covering the spider. 'The name's Bo. I'm a spy for Her Majesty's Secret Service,' he said.

I laughed. Now I understood. This was a DREAM, a fun one that I could take part in until I woke up. So I said, 'You're a spy?'

'Of course not!' Bo cackled. 'I was only joking. I wish I was a spy, though.'

'How come I can hear you?'

Bo swivelled his head left, and then right, like he was an undercover spy and was checking no one could overhear. 'Through the Slugs. They're magic.'

'No!'

'Yes!'

I yanked out the Slugs while he was still talking to me. All I heard was

Chirp! Chirp! Chirp!

When I put them back in again, I heard Bo cackling, 'Magic! I tell you!'

OK. Maybe this wasn't a dream. This was FOR REAL. My fingers tingled with excitement. 'Magic, like a spell?' I asked him.

'I don't know,' said Bo.

'Or magic like a potion?

'I don't know,' said Bo, again.

'Can anyone wearing Slugs hear you?'

'I don't know,' said Bo, again.

'Can I hear you if you're in the sky?'

'I don't know,' said Bo, again.

'You don't know very much, do you?'

'Puh.' Bo ruffled his feathers. 'I DO know

that Arthur said it was magic and that magic only happens to special people.'

'Who's Arthur?'

'My owner. Grand old fella, he was. We talked all the time when I lived with him.'

'So why aren't you living with Arthur anymore?' I asked.

Bo went quiet and studied his claws. Eventually, he looked up and said, 'Arthur died.'

'That's so sad.' Poor Bo!

Bo nodded his little head. 'Arthur's family broke their promise to look after me. They said I was stinky and dumb and they didn't want me because I didn't copy them like a parrot.' Bo ruffled his feathers. 'I talk much better than a parrot,' he said indignantly. 'Anyway, have you got any food? I'm starving!'

Just then, Luke ran into the den. 'Who are you talking to?' he asked.

'The bird.' I pointed at Bo.

'Don't be silly!' said Luke.

'Don't be silly!' Bo copied.

I giggled, thankful that Luke couldn't hear Bo's mimicking. All he could hear was

Chirp! Chirp! Chirp!

Luke looked confused. 'What's funny?'

'Nothing. What's for tea?'

'Sausages,' said Luke.

'Sausages!' Bo repeated. 'I love sausages.'

Bo was so funny I couldn't stop laughing.

'But that's not the most importantest thing. Guess what? Mum's bike has gone missing!' said Luke. 'She rode it to the station and parked it there and locked it up and everything. Then she caught the train to work and a baddie took it.'

Another case for the SPUD!

'Mum is very, very cross,' said Luke.

'Very, very cross,' copied Bo.

That gave me the giggles again.

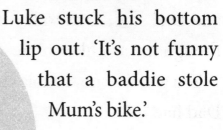

Luke stuck his bottom lip out. 'It's not funny that a baddie stole Mum's bike.'

'I'm not laughing at that,' I said.

'It's not funny!' Bo mimicked, except he was extra funny because he spoke like a cartoon queen with a peg on her nose.

'Shut up!' I said to Bo.

But Luke thought I was telling him to shut up and he ran off to tell Dad. Then Dad came out and it was obvious he was in a bad mood about Mum's bike.

'There's no need to be rude to Luke,' he said.

I couldn't explain that I was telling a bird to shut up, could I? So I apologised and Dad said I had to lay the table, even though it was Luke's turn.

'You got me into trouble,' I told Bo, when Dad had gone.

'Sorry,' said Bo.

'That's OK. We just have to be careful only to talk when we're alone.' I stroked Bo's warm head and he nestled against my hand. This was the most amazing thing that had ever happened to me!

SPUD CASE FILE: Missing Thing #4

Crime: Theft of Mum's mountain bike.

Location: Bike rack at the train station.

Description: Blue with lots of scratches. Wicker basket on the front.

Action: Examination of scene for clues. Padlock was broken using strong cutters.

Suspects: Police said a suspect was seen on CCTV cutting bike lock and riding away. Bearded man wearing a hoodie.

7

The Spy in the Sky

'I hereby announce this meeting of Super Perceptive Undercover Detectives open,' Grace said. She sat down on the bedroom floor next to me and turned to a clean page in our SPUD logbook. 'First, we need an update on all of our cases.'

'Luke's swimming trunks are still missing,' I reported. 'So is Mrs Moore's mountain bike and the school's tractor mower.'

'There's your mum's bike, too,' said Grace.

'Mum's just come back from the police station and they told her there've been three more thefts reported.' It took ages to get more details because she was so angry while telling Mrs Moore about it that I couldn't get a word in edgeways or upside down or any way at all.

Chirp! Chirp! Chirp!

'Oh, look, that mynah bird's back again,' said Grace.

'I'm hungry,' Bo squawked.

I bit one of my grapes in half and placed it on the windowsill for him.

'Yum!'

Grace chewed the end of her pencil. 'I think there's a link between all the cases,' she said. 'They're all thefts and they all happened when the owners had left the items unwatched.'

I studied the case notes. 'A lot of the missing things have been stolen from Market Square. Two scooters from outside the chippie and a mountain bike from the railings by the library.'

Next we wrote a list of questions.

SPUD CASE FILE:

Where do thieves hide stolen things? It needs to be somewhere large because a tractor mower is too big to hide in a coat cupboard or under the stairs.

A lot of the missing things have been stolen from the Market Square. Is this a pattern?

Does the thief (or thieves?) spy on people riding bikes and scooters?

'We need a plan,' Grace declared.

'I think we should set up camp in Market Square,' I said. 'When we see someone leave their bike or scooter outside a shop we need to watch to see if anyone tries to steal it.'

'Then we can ring the police using our mobile phones,' said Grace. 'That counts as an extreme emergency, right?'

'It's a big extreme emergency,' I agreed. 'We'll have to hide where we can see the suspects but they can't see us.'

'We need eyes everywhere!' Grace laughed.

Bo hopped up and down on the windowsill. 'Me! Me! I can be the spy in the sky!'

'That's an amazing idea!' I said.

Grace looked confused. 'What is?'

I looked at Bo. 'Can I tell her?'

'Tell me what?' Grace demanded, looking even more puzzled.

Bo cocked his head on one side. 'Can she keep a secret?'

'Yes.'

Bo nodded, which looked quite funny because his head bobbed up and down, and then returned to pecking at the grape.

'I'm going to tell you the biggest secret ever,' I said to Grace. 'Pinky promise you'll keep it?'

'Pinky promise,' she replied.

Grace's eyes bulged as I told her everything about Bo. 'Can I try the Slugs?'

I didn't know if I was allowed to share them because of germs and stuff but this was a special circumstance.

'They feel really weird and everything's so loud!' Grace looked at Bo and said, 'Hello Bo!'

Chirp! Chirp! Chirp!

Her smile disappeared and she looked upset.

'All I can hear is Chirp! Chirp! Chirp!'

I wiped the Slugs and put them back into my ears.

Straightaway Bo said, 'I like her. I wish she could hear me.'

I reported back to Grace.

Bo hopped onto Grace's hand and chirped. She smiled at Bo. 'At least we can still talk to each other if Callie's here to translate for us.'

So now there were three of us in the SPUD crew – and we had a mission to carry out!

MISSION: To spy on potential suspects.

Agents: Callie Major, Grace Ambrose, Bo Mynah.

Equipment: Binoculars, camera, notebook, mobile phone, CCTV picture of suspect.

Plan: Set up camp in village square. Hide where we can see suspects but make sure we stay OUT OF SIGHT.

SPUD Crew in Action

Grace and I chained our bikes to the railings by the glass-recycling skip and hid behind a prickly hedge next to the library. Bo flew onto the library roof.

Me: Can you hear me?

Bo: Message received!

Me: How cool is that?! What can you see?

Bo: Shops. Cars. People. Ooooh, a hotdog stand!

Me: Bo, focus! Can you see the bicycle thief?

Bo: Negative.

We spied for ages. We saw a man riding a bike while taking a humungous dog for a walk; our postie, Jane, who runs Beavers and has spiky blue hair which I love. And then…

Bo: Suspect alert. New sighting. Man. Bushy beard. Grey hoodie.

Me: Does it look like the man in the police photo?

Bo: Affirmative.

Me: Is he on his own?

Bo: Looks like it. He's coming this way!

Grace and I ducked behind the bush but we kept our eyes trained on him through our binoculars. We held our breath, trying not to move a muscle. Then he sat on the bench almost in front of us and opened a magazine. We knew it was a cover and really he was spying because he kept looking up and he never turned the page over. That's a BIG giveaway.

We watched the suspect for ages. He was there for so long that Grace's tummy rumbled! He got up so suddenly I wondered if he'd heard it too. Luckily, he turned and walked across the square to the chippie.

Bo: I love chips.

Me: This isn't the time to think about food.

Grace and I crept out from behind the prickly bush and followed him. My heart thumped like the big bass drum we've got at school.

Grace gasped. 'He's stealing the scooter left outside the chippie!'

A crime right in front of our eyes!

'Let's follow him!' I said.

Then there was lots of noise and confusion because a woman ran out of the chippie and shouted at the thief. He threw the scooter down and ran away.

Me: Follow him, Bo!

Bo: Spy in the Sky is on the case!

Grace and I ran to fetch our bikes and discovered a disaster ... our back tyres were flat.

Was it a huge coincidence? Or was the thief on to us?

Bo: Suspect running along Station Road.

Me: Keep following!

Bo: Affirmative ... he's very quick ... a train is pulling into the station ... oh...

Me: Oh what? Bo? Bo?

Bo: Suspect on train. Can't see him anymore.

Grace and I swapped a glance. We both knew the trail had gone cold.

Me: You did your best. Fly back to mine and we'll meet you there.

A Different Crime

At home, Dad took the inner tube out of my bike's back tyre.

'It's got a puncture. Look, there's a shard of glass embedded into it.' He frowned. 'Where did you go?'

'Just to the Market Square,' I said.

'Did you go anywhere near the recycling skips? The ones next to the library?'

I nodded.

Dad pulled the piece of glass out of the rubber tyre. 'Here's the culprit. Sometimes glass bottles get dropped when people are putting them in the recycling skip, or bottles fall out and break on the ground when the skip is being changed,' he said. 'I think that's where the glass came from.'

We'd have to remember this for future missions.

Dad offered to repair Grace's back tyre, too, because he's kind like that. While we were waiting, Mum asked if she'd be able to ride my bike to the station for a while, until the police found hers or she bought another one. 'Otherwise I'll have to walk every day and it'll take ages,' she said.

So I moved the seat and the handlebars as high as they'd go.

'Try it out,' I said.

Mum wobbled a bit as she climbed on. Bo flew on to my shoulder to watch. He tucked in his wings but his feathers kept tickling my neck.

'And she's off … approaching the first fence … in the lead by a head … three furlongs to go…' said Bo.

'What are you talking about?' I whispered.

'Horse racing. Arthur loved it. Watched it on the telly every afternoon, we did.' Bo sighed. 'He used to read me stories, too.'

'You miss Arthur a lot,' I said.

Bo didn't answer. He buried his head in my neck instead.

Mum pulled on the brakes and came to a stop right next to us, without falling off. 'Well, it's a little bit smaller than I'm used to, but it'll be much better than walking every day!' She looked at Bo on my shoulder. 'That bird is very tame.'

'He's a mynah bird. I looked it up. He's definitely been abandoned.'

'How do you know that?' asked Mum.

'I've been watching him. He's not a wild

bird because he's rubbish at finding his own food.'

'Oi!' Bo squawked.

Bo hopped on to the bike's handlebars and looked at Mum. 'Can I live here?' he asked her.

Of course, all Mum heard was

Chirp! Chirp! Chirp!

'I think you're right. Wild birds aren't that tame,' she said.

So then Bo rubbed his head against her hand. I braced myself for her reaction but Mum didn't shriek about being allergic or anything!

'He is quite sweet,' Mum admitted.

I grinned. 'Can we keep him? Please? I'll be responsible for him,' I promised. Adults like it when you use the word

RESPONSIBLE because it's grown-up and sounds like you really mean it. Which I DO.

Eventually, Mum said, 'I'll think about it.'

Which was better than 'no'.

Dad mended the punctures quickly because we had to go to school – on a Saturday! – for a special crime-prevention day run by the police.

Grace and I got to ride our bikes around the playground which was cool because normally it was banned. Then the police officer used a special marker to put a number on our bike frames. That way, anyone who wanted to buy a second-hand bike could check it wasn't listed on the police database as stolen.

A policewoman gave out leaflets about security, as well as a poster about the bicycle thief with the fuzzy CCTV photo.

'From that photo, it could be anyone,'
Dad said.

'Keep an eye out. The thief will need
somewhere to hide the stolen goods until

they can sell them on.' She held up a poster which said LOCK IT OR LOSE IT.

Luke frowned. 'My mum did lock her bike and it still got stolen.'

'That was very unlucky,' said the police officer.

'That's not the word my mum used,' said Luke. 'She said—'

'Yes, well, must be off,' said Dad, and he hurried us away before Luke repeated the EXACT rude word Mum had used.

When we got home, Dad unlocked the side gate so we could take our bikes to the shed in the garden without wheeling them through the house.

'Daaaad! There's a bird eating your blackcurrants,' Luke shouted.

I ran into the garden and saw Bo in Dad's blackcurrant bush.

Dad ran around shouting. 'Shoo! Shoo!'

Bo screeched and flew away.

'You've scared him now!' I huffed.

'It was eating my blackcurrants!'

'That's because he's hungry!'

Mum came into the garden and told Dad about me wanting to keep Bo. It was the worst time ever for her to say anything because Dad was still cross about the blackcurrants, so he said 'no'.

'We could get a bird feeder,' Mum suggested.

'No! I don't want to encourage more birds to the garden. I want them all to go away!' Dad bellowed.

But I wasn't going to give up. I just needed to find another food source for Bo. What I needed was … WORMS.

Worms

'Worms?' Bo blinked. 'What are worms?'

'Wriggly creatures. You eat them. Mynah birds love them, it says so on the wild birds website,' I said.

'Arthur didn't give me worms.' Bo burped. It smelled of blackcurrants.

Then there was a **SPLODGE**.

And another **SPLODGE**.

SPLODGE SPLODGE SPLODGE.

'Yuck!' Grace wrinkled her nose. 'That's disgusting … and very purple.'

We used tissues to wipe off the purple poo splattered on my windowsill.

'Bo, we really want you to be our Spy in the Sky, but you must follow the rules,' I told him.

'What rules?'

'Rule number one is no blackcurrants!'

Bo groaned. 'Not even one tiny, weeny one? They're so scrumptious!'

I shook my head. 'Not even one. You need to find something different to eat. Like worms.'

'There are loads of worms in the compost heap at the bottom of our garden,' said Grace.

'I think you should try some,' I told Bo.

'Puh!' Bo sniffed.

The compost heap in Grace's back garden was a mini mountain of mouldy plants and bits of food and brown grass cuttings. Shimmers of heat rose out of it when we poked it with sticks. This was because there were lots of organic things going rotten in there which were making chemicals. I knew because Mrs Manning told us when we did our Green Watch project last term.

'Pongy pongy pongy!' Bo squawked.

I dug a spade into the heap and found loads of wriggly worms. I held out the spade. 'Have a worm.'

Bo prodded it with his orange beak. The worm wriggled some more. Then Bo sucked it into his beak at supersonic speed. Afterwards, he gave a huge, birdy BURP.

'More worms!' he chirped.

I picked bits of stinky compost off my legs. 'You're a bird,' I reminded him. 'The idea is that you find them on your own.'

Bo looked at the steaming compost heap.

BUUURRRP

Bo Breaks the Rules

At lunchtime on Monday we had a Bike Club meeting at school. Grace and I love Bike Club because we get to ride our bikes to different places. Our meeting was about our summer party. We get to ride around the gardens at a huge mansion and we're allowed to swim in the pool. Afterwards we have a picnic but I'll only be able to go if we find Mum's bike. Otherwise, she'll have to borrow mine so she can get to work.

'That gives us four days,' said Grace.

We decided to hold another spying mission in the Market Square after school. Dad collected us and I was just about to ask permission to go out with Grace when he glanced out of the kitchen window and yelled, 'Not again!'

Dad ran into the garden and flapped his arms around like a scarecrow blowing in the wind.

Oh no! Bo hadn't eaten just one or two of Dad's blackcurrants.

Or even three or four.

He'd eaten ALL of them.

Bo perched on the patio table. His belly bulged. 'I feel sick,' he moaned.

'Hmm,' I said. I sounded just like Mum when Luke and I have done something bad, but I felt really sorry for Dad. He'd worked for ages in the garden and because of Bo he wouldn't get to try even one blackcurrant. I felt sorry for Bo, too. It wasn't his fault he'd been abandoned and didn't know how to survive in the wild.

Luke grabbed his lightsaber and charged at Bo. 'Zzzhoooom. Zzzhoooom.'

'Leave him alone!' I shouted.

But Luke was too busy saving the world from one scared bird to listen to me. So I grabbed him.

Then Luke fell over.

And trod on his Superman cape.

And tore it.

And apparently it was ALL MY FAULT.

We had a big argument and Dad sent me to my room to calm down. That made me even angrier. All I cared about was Bo. I kept calling him from my bedroom window but he didn't come. Maybe his belly was so heavy he couldn't fly? I wanted to search for him but Dad said I was grounded.

That night I kept waking up because I was so worried. I opened the bedroom window to call him. I even used my torch, which made the garden look spooky with lots of weird shadows.

The next morning, while Dad and Luke were brushing their teeth before we went to school, I sneaked into the garden.

'Bo! Bo? Bo, where are you?' I called.

Nothing.

My tummy twisted in a painful knot.

Bo was missing!

SPUD CASE FILE: Missing Thing #5

Crime: Disappearance of <u>Bo</u> aka: <u>The Spy</u>
<u>in the Sky.</u>

Description: A black mynah bird with
yellow stripes on its head. Orange beak.
Bigger than a robin but smaller than a
crow. Always hungry.

Last seen: Back garden of 20 Merton Way.

Action: Launch an investigation.

Suspects: None.

Operation Bo

'We need to launch a search!' Grace declared.

I nodded. I'd been worried all day about Bo while I was at school. I didn't even want to play tag with Jack, Finn and Grace. I'd rushed into the garden the moment we got home from school and called Bo, but he was still missing.

'The first thing to do is examine the crime area for clues,' said Grace. 'That's what real detectives do. I saw it on TV.'

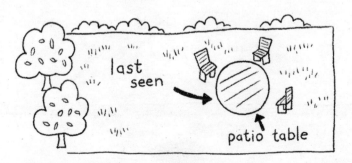

last seen

patio table

I trained my binoculars around the garden and in all the fir trees. Nothing.

'Let's go to my house,' Grace suggested. 'We can see things from a different angle from my bedroom.'

Grace's house is the same shape as ours and she shares it with her mum, dad, and her twin brothers. Zeb and Noah are in Year 9 and they're really tall and into gaming. They're so much cooler than Luke, who is being such a baby about the ripped Superman cape thing.

Grace's mum poured us some mango juice and we took it up to Grace's bedroom. I spied through the binoculars and Grace wrote notes.

I saw Luke's frisbee on Mr Wilson's shed roof...

A new trampoline in Millie's garden...

Beautiful pink roses in the garden at Number 12...

But still no Bo.

Grace chewed the end of her pencil, which she did a lot when she was thinking. 'We need to widen the search area. I'll draw a map.'

'Let's go to search area number one first,' I decided. It made sense because it was closest to our house.

We grabbed our binoculars and walked along the footpath. The bushes were very bushy and it felt so creepy I wouldn't have been surprised to bump into a witch or a mythical creature from a faraway land. Grace and I kept our eyes peeled for evidence of Bo or anything unusual.

'Is Bo small enough to get stuck in one of those cracks?' asked Grace.

We both bent down to investigate. The ground was covered in zig-zag cracks because of the heatwave. I measured the gap with my fingers.

'It's too small,' I decided. 'Even if he was, he'd cry for help.' I hated that I couldn't hear him. My tummy did its madly spinning washing-machine thing.

'Look!' Grace pointed at a trail of purple bird poo on the ground.

I squatted down and examined it with a stick. 'It's gooey and hasn't had time to dry so Bo must have been here recently. There's some more over there.'

We followed the trail of purple poo to the end of the footpath and then out to the playing fields, where it stopped.

'Maybe he was all poo-ed out?' said Grace.

We took a few steps further. Then I saw something red in the bush which looked familiar...

Luke's swimming trunks!

'What are they doing there?' said Grace.

Grace pushed the leaves aside and I leaned in to pull the trunks out. They were splattered in purple poo and smelled of Bo.

'Bo must have taken them from our washing line. It looks like he's used them as a bed,' I said.

'Maybe that's why he ran away, because he stole them as well as your dad's blackcurrants?' Grace wondered. 'I'll put them in my bag as evidence.'

'Grace, look! Feathers.' I pointed at the grassy track just ahead of us. Two black feathers and one yellow one, EXACTLY the same colour as the splash of yellow on Bo's head. 'And look, here … it looks like cat fur.'

My tummy lurched and felt even worse than a spinning washing machine. It was more like a great big cement mixer. Something was wrong. I was sure of it. We knelt down and studied the evidence.

'I think Bo has had a fight with a cat.' My voice went wobbly as I blinked back tears.

'I think you're right,' said Grace.

So, we'd solved the mystery of one of the missing things. But where was Bo? Was he hurt?

Or even worse?

Detectives at Work

Grace and I rode around all the search areas. We looked out for all the places he might be. I wasn't sure how close Bo needed to be to hear me, but I called him anyway. I told him he wasn't in trouble and to come home. Maybe he was too far away to hear me? The only difference was that I heard a strange beeping noise. Grace couldn't hear it so it must be coming from the Slugs.

It was impossible. There were zillions of trees in our village. We never realised how many there were. Tall. Short. Bushy. Skinny. All places Bo could be hiding.

Or lying hurt. We decided to go home and come up with plan B.

'We need to think like detectives,' said Grace. 'Where else would Bo go?'

I twisted my bead bracelet into a knot. 'His old house is locked up and for sale, and I don't know where it is, anyway.'

'Is there someone else he could go to?' asked Grace.

'Bo didn't talk about anyone else. His whole world had been Arthur.' I sighed. And then I had a brainwave. 'That's it! Arthur. Bo would have gone to Arthur.'

'But Arthur's dead...' said Grace, looking confused.

'Yes. We need to find out where he's buried,' I said.

'But we don't know Arthur's surname or anything,' said Grace.

'Oh!' I jumped up. 'The local newspaper! That's what we need.'

But when we went downstairs to find this week's copy of *The Messenger* we found Mum reading it.

'I'm trying to find a second-hand bike for sale but I'm not having much luck,' she said.

'We're looking for a dead man,' I told her.

Mum looked at me like I was bonkers. 'Why?'

'Because we're being detectives,' I replied, which was the truth. 'We're not going to get into trouble or anything, I promise.'

'OK.' Mum rifled through the newspaper. 'Here, this is the funeral notices column. It lists all the local people who've died and when their funeral service will be.'

I ran my finger down the column. The entries were in alphabetical order but I had to read every single one because I didn't know Arthur's surname. I was quite surprised at how many people in our local area had died. Unfortunately, none of them was called Arthur so we had to rummage through the recycling sack to find last week's newspaper. We took it to my bedroom to read.

'I think I've found it!' said Grace. 'This is the only Arthur so it must be him.'

MAXTED, Arthur, aged 88 years. Loving husband of the late Gwen. Funeral service and burial to take place at All Saint's Parish Church, Hurst, on Monday 13th June.

I looked at my Amazing Tarantulas calendar. This Arthur's funeral had taken place the day before I'd gone to the hospital to collect the Slugs. Bo had said his Arthur was an old man, so the age fitted.

'It's got to be Bo's Arthur,' I said.

'Let's go to the churchyard right now,' Grace replied.

The Slugs made the strange beeping noise again, but I didn't have time to worry about that now. We got on our bikes but then Dad came running out. 'Can you pop to the shop for some sugar and milk, please?'

'Sure,' I said.

We raced up the hill to the church because we wanted to get there as quickly as possible. But it felt wrong to ride in the churchyard, so we got off and pushed our bikes instead. The graveyard was behind the church, on a slope. Some of the graves were overgrown and their stones leaned at an angle. The gravestones were shiny white marble or simple slabs of grey stone, and they all had words carved into them. I read one of them.

'The man buried here died in 1864,' I said.

'That's more than one hundred and fifty years ago,' Grace worked out. 'We need to find the newer graves.'

We headed further away from the church towards a stone wall at the edge of the graveyard. I called out for Bo all the time but the only sounds I heard were the irritating beeps. I used my binoculars to look at an ancient yew tree that looked like it might topple in the slightest puff of wind. Bo wasn't hiding in there either.

Then I saw two new

graves, one near the hedge and another next to an older grave. The one near the hedge had a bunch of withered flowers on top of it and a black plastic name sign:

Florence Dryer, aged 94 years

"This isn't him,' said Grace. 'What about the other one?'

I read the sign by the second grave: Arthur Maxted, aged 88 years. 'We've found Arthur!'

'But where's Bo?' asked Grace.

'Bo! Bo!' I called. No Bo. Only more stupid beeps coming from the Slugs. I didn't know what to do. I was SO sure we'd find him here. I was NEVER going to see

Bo again. I sat down next to Arthur's grave and picked at the grass. I didn't care if anyone saw me crying. That's what people did in churchyards anyway.

'We need you, Bo,' I said aloud, even though he wasn't there to hear me. 'You're our secret weapon. We can't crack the case without you. But also, you're funny and cute and I miss you.'

'I miss you loads too,' said Grace.

Then I felt something warm and soft tickling my neck. What? Was it really…

'Bo! You're alive!'

'Of course I'm alive. Wasn't going to let a miserable cat get me.' He snorted, which made me giggle. 'Why are you crying?'

'Because I thought I'd never see you again.'

Bo nuzzled my neck. 'I thought you wouldn't want me anymore because I got you into trouble again.'

'I'll never abandon you, Bo,' I promised. 'Tell us what happened.'

'I was chilling out in a tree and a cat attacked me. How rude was that? I had to fight it off.' Bo hissed but it was a rubbish cat impression. He showed us the deep scratch marks on his head where the cat had clawed him.

'That was a lucky escape,' said Grace.

'I'm not very good at being wild,' said Bo.

'You should have built your nest higher up. Then the cat wouldn't have been able to reach you,' I said.

'I know that now,' Bo huffed, and he sounded much more like his normal self. 'I decided to come up here, say goodbye to my Arthur but I can't read so I don't know which grave is his.'

I pointed to it.

Arthur Maxted,
aged 88 years

Bo hopped on to the mound of earth. He sat there for a while, in silence, and closed his eyes. I sat next to him. After some time, Bo rubbed his head against the earth and chirped sadly. Then he jumped on to my shoulder and brushed his head against my neck.

My mobile phone buzzed in my pocket.

Dad: Where is the sugar & milk?

Oops! I'd completely forgotten about the shopping! Grace and I whizzed down the hill to the shops. Bo flew alongside me. It made me feel like I was flying, too! But I wished the Slugs would stop beeping.

We locked our bikes to the railings outside the shop and rushed in to buy the sugar and milk. More beeps went off in my ear, which was really annoying.

'I'm so happy we found Bo,' said Grace.

'Me too, but I don't think my dad will let him live with us. Not after the blackcurrant incident,' I said.

Bo: Emergency! SOS! Alert! Alert!

Me: Bo! What is it?

Bo: The thief is stealing Grace's bike!

The Flying Detective

We dumped the sugar and milk on the counter and ran out, which really confused the shop assistant. We didn't have time to explain because the thief was already riding off with Grace's bike!

Bo: I am the Spy in the Sky.

Me: Grace is ringing the police. I'll catch up with you and take photos of the suspect for evidence. Where are you?

Bo: Tracking suspect. High Street.
    Heading east towards the station.

I pedalled as fast as I could. The Slugs
beeped again. Then they cut out for a few
seconds. What was going on?

Me: Can you hear me?

Bo: Affirmative.

Me: I lost you there for a bit.

Bo: Ooh. Ice cream van! I love ice cream.

    Especially the chocolate flake thingy.

Me: Bo! Watch the thief!

Bo: Tracking suspect. Approaching traffic lights. Suspect at crossroads.

Me: Message received.

Bo: Suspect turning—

Me: Suspect turning where?

Silence.

Me: Bo! Can you hear me?

Silence. Not even the beeps were beeping now. Far too late, I realised what the beeping noises were. It was the Slugs, warning me that their batteries were wearing out. And now it was too late because the Slugs were DEAD!

Emergency

This was a disaster!

Don't panic. That was the first rule of being a detective (well, it might have been the second or third but I wasn't going to worry about it right then).

Think!

I needed new batteries for the Slugs and they were at home. I rang Grace to tell her what had happened. She ran back to my house and I rode faster than I ever have in my whole entire life. We arrived at the same time.

Dad was trimming the hedge in the front garden. 'What's the rush?' he asked.

'I need new batteries for the Slugs so I can hear,' I gasped.

'I thought you hated the Slugs.'

'I do. And I don't.'

'You are a contrary child,' he declared.

Which sounded cool even if I wasn't a hundred per cent sure what it meant.

Grace managed to persuade Luke to let her borrow his scooter. I put the new batteries into the Slugs.

Me: Bo, can you hear me?

Bo: Affirmative. What happened?

Me: Long story. Where are you?

Bo: A road somewhere.

Me: Which one?

Bo: How would I know? I'm a talking
    bird. Not a reading bird!

Me: What can you see?

Bo: Long flat building. Empty car park,
    covered in stinging nettles.

My mind raced as I tried to picture
where he was.

Me: Can you see the railway?

Bo: Affirmative.

Me: You're at the industrial estate!

Grace rang the police again, who said they would send out an emergency response team to the industrial estate. Grace and I set off, too. Grace was really whizzy on Luke's scooter and, because we're a team, I cycled slower so we stayed together.

Bo: Tracking suspect.

Me: We're nearly there.

Bo: Target ... fire!

Me: What are you doing?

Bo: Fire! Fire! Fire!

Me: There's a fire?

Grace looked very alarmed as I told her what Bo had shouted. My heart thumped as we zoomed along Stanley Street and Bathurst Road, and then into the industrial estate on the outskirts of the village. Some of the buildings were modern but they were next to an empty old car park covered in stinging nettles and old huts that looked abandoned. We used our binoculars but we couldn't see a fire anywhere.

'There's the thief! With my bike!' Grace shouted, pointing towards the old huts. 'Bo is splattering him with purple poo!'

So that was what Bo had meant – he was FIRING poo at the thief!

Then the police arrived. Thanks to Bo we could show them EXACTLY where the thief was. They chased him in their car with the sirens BLARING. He dumped Grace's bike and jumped over a low wall.

'He's going to get away!' shouted Grace.

Bo swooped down and divebombed the thief.

The thief tried to swipe him out of the way, but Bo was too quick for him.

'Help!' shouted the thief.

Bo swooped again.

SPLAT!

SPLAT!

SPLAT!

A huge dollop of purple poo landed on the thief's face.

A police officer grabbed him. 'You've been caught purple-handed,' she said, chuckling.

16

A New Start

The police had been on the thief's tail as well, but Bo beat them to it and made their job much easier. They found the lock-up garage on the industrial estate where the thief had stored all the stolen things. Everything was returned to the rightful owners. Mum got her bike back. Grace and I toasted SPUD's success with a can of lemonade each. Afterwards, I was allowed to sit on the sofa in our living room ... WITH BO!

'You're a hero,' I told him.

'Hero!' he mumbled. Then he tucked his head into my neck and snored!

'In a roundabout way, Dad, your blackcurrants helped to catch the thief,' I said.

Dad looked confused until I told him about the purple poo.

'Hmm…' said Dad.

There was other good news, too. Mum didn't need to borrow my bike anymore which meant I could go to the Bike Club summer party. Luke was happy because Mum bought him a new pair of swimming trunks with an alien on them. The best part was that Mum and Dad have agreed that Bo can live with us!

'You mustn't get bored and abandon him, like some people do with cats and dogs they're given as presents at Christmas,' Mum warned.

'I promise I'll look after him and I'll keep him away from Dad's fruit and vegetable patch.' Of course, Mum and Dad have no idea that Bo and I can talk to each other.

Dad said he would build Bo a special bird house out of wood as long as I promise to wear the Slugs, even when I don't want to.

Bo woke up suddenly and shot outside. We all followed him and found a huge splat of purple poo on the patio.

'Bo!' said Mum, pretending to be OUTRAGED.

But I knew he'd won her over. Now he was a member of our family!

SPUD CASE FILE: Final Report

Case ref no: SPUD-004

Agents: CM1

GA1

Spy in the Sky

Crime: Theft of five mountain bikes, school
tractor mower and four scooters.

Location: Various places around the village.

Action: Examination of scenes for clues.

Speaking to witnesses.

Surveillance.

Outcome: Suspect observed while committing a crime
and followed until police arrived.

Stolen items returned to rightful owners.

SOLVED!

CALLIE

GRACE

BO

THIEF

Coming Spring 2023:

a new

MAJOR
and
MyNAH

adventure

Karen Owen

Karen loved books from a young age and read every children's title in the village library. She spends her days in a variety of imaginary worlds, either writing or reading. Her favourite story is always the one she's creating at the moment. She enjoys hiking and her ambition is to walk the entire coastline of Britain (but not all in one go).

Louise Forshaw

Louise Forshaw is an illustrator from the North East, living just outside Newcastle upon Tyne. She lives with her fiancé and three noisy Jack Russell terriers. To date, Louise has illustrated over seventy children's books. When she's not drawing, Louise loves watching animated films, adding to her over-flowing 'to be read' pile and reading lots of books.

Acknowledgements

Karen Owen:

Creating this story in my imagination was a lot of fun. Getting it down on the page was much harder and here I'd like to thank my wonderfully inspiring and supportive crew of fellow writers who read various drafts, especially Julie Fulton, Sarah Mussi and Margaret Bateson-Hill. Thanks to editor Leonie Lock, who championed Callie et al from the first time she read about their exploits, and to illustrator Louise Forshaw, whose drawings bring life to the page.

But my biggest thanks go to the many dedicated ENT doctors whose exceptional skills over the years have safeguarded my limited hearing. I am forever grateful.

Louise Forshaw:

A huge thank you to my amazing agent Bhavisha Vadgama, who is forever supportive and encouraging. Thanks also to the brilliant team at Firefly, especially Leonie Lock and Becka Moor for choosing me as illustrator. Also to Karen Owen, for creating such a fun story that I feel honoured to illustrate. Last but not least, the biggest thank you goes to all the wonderful readers out there. Keep reading!

All About Hearing Loss

Our ears are AMAZING things. The human ear has three parts and they work together as a team so that we can hear.

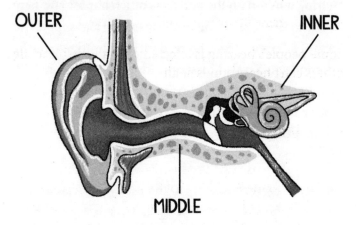

OUTER · INNER · MIDDLE

The outer ear picks up sound waves that travel through the ear canal to the middle ear.

When the sound waves hit the ear drum in the middle ear, the ear drum vibrates and three tiny bones move. They help sound travel to the inner ear.

The vibrations move to the cochlear, which is lined with tiny hairs. These hairs fine tune the sound waves and turn them into electronic signals. The hearing nerves send these to the brain and then you can hear.

What Can Go Wrong?

Hearing loss happens when there's a problem with part of the ear or the hearing part of our brain.

Some children are born with hearing loss. Others develop it as they grow up or when they're adults.

Some people's hearing is affected only a little bit while others can't hear sounds at all.

What Can Doctors Do?

Doctors can use special hearing tests, like the ones Callie has in the beginning of this book, to find out the type of hearing loss and what is causing it. Then they can prescribe medicine or perform an operation. There are hearing aids which make sounds louder, and other listening gadgets to use at school and home.

What Else Is There?

Some children with hearing loss learn to read people's lips while they talk. This helps them to understand what's being said. Others learn sign language, which is a way of communicating with your hands instead of speaking.

Make Your Own Compost!

Bo is a big fan of wriggly worms that live in the compost heap in Grace's garden. Here's Grace to tell us how to make our own compost and why it's important for our planet.

Nature is brilliant at recycling leaves and plants into new food for plants called compost. It's really easy to make some in your garden or at school.

Before you begin, make sure to ask permission from a responsible adult.

You will need:

- A wooden or plastic box with a hole in the bottom

- Some brown stuff (like dead, dried plants or leaves)

- Some green stuff (like freshly cut grass, banana peel, apple cores, or other peelings from the kitchen

- Some water

- Soil to sprinkle

Great! Now you have all you need, just follow these steps:

1. First, recycle a wooden or plastic box and find a place to put it that's out of the way. Make a big hole in the bottom so that worms can get in and rain water can drain out.

2. Next, you need to feed the compost bin. The micro-organisms that recycle leaves and plants need food to munch on. This is the brown stuff and the green stuff. It also needs water and air.

Start with a layer of the brown stuff and spread it evenly. Give this a drink of water so it's all a bit soggy. Then feed it a layer of the green stuff and give it another drink!

3. Sprinkle a generous layer of soil on top.

4. Then add more layers of brown stuff, water, and green stuff.

5. Now leave your box in its new home, and wash your hands! The composting has begun!

The micro-organisms from the soil you added soon get to work. They're breaking down the brown and green stuff into compost.

While this is slowly happening, other living things are moving in to live in the compost bin, such as millipedes and the worms that Bo loves.

Each week, turn over all the brown and green stuff with a garden fork. This adds air to everything, which is another vital ingredient.

It takes months for your compost to be made so you'll have to be patient! When it's ready, it looks like dark earth and it is rich in nutrients. You can mix it into the soil to feed your plants or when you are planting new flowers or vegetables.

See, nature is brilliant at recycling!

Environmental statement

At Firefly we care very much about the environment and our responsibility to it.

Many of our stories, such as this one, involve the natural world, our place in it and what we can all do to help it, and us, survive the challenges of the climate emergency. Go to our website **www.fireflypress.co.uk** to find more of our great stories that focus on the environment, like *The Territory*, *Aubrey and the Terrible Ladybirds*, *The Song that Sings Us* and *My Name is River*.

As a Wales-based publisher we are also very proud of the beautiful natural places, plants and animals in our country on the western side of Great Britain.

We are always looking at reducing our impact on the environment, including our carbon footprint and the materials we use, and are taking part in UK-wide publishing initiatives to improve this wherever we can.

BUUURRRP